For Jill – L.H.

First published in Great Britain 2022 by Farshore
An imprint of HarperCollins*Publishers*
1 London Bridge Street, London SE1 9GF
www.farshore.co.uk

HarperCollins*Publishers*
1st Floor, Watermarque Building, Ringsend Road
Dublin 4, Ireland

Text copyright © Juno Dawson 2022
Illustrations copyright © Laura Hughes 2022
Juno Dawson and Laura Hughes have asserted their moral rights.

HB ISBN 978 0 00 850093 1
PB ISBN 978 0 00 848828 4
Printed in Italy.
001

A CIP catalogue record for this title is available from the British Library.

Stay safe online. Any website addresses listed in this book are correct at the time
of going to print. However, Farshore is not responsible for content hosted by
third parties. Please be aware that online content can be subject to change
and websites can contain content that is unsuitable for children.
We advise that all children are supervised when using the internet.

MIX
Paper | Supporting
responsible forestry
FSC™ C007454

This book is produced from independently certified FSC™ paper
to ensure responsible forest management.

For more information visit: www.harpercollins.co.uk/green

YOU NEED TO Chill!

JUNO DAWSON

ILLUSTRATED BY LAURA HUGHES

Farshore

Sometimes people say to me:
"What happened to your brother Bill?

We haven't seen him in ages.
Is he hiding?
Is he ill?"

"Is he lost in the park?

Is he scared of the dark?

Is he doing his homework still?"

That's when I look them in the eye and say:
"Hun, you need to chill."

"Was he eaten by a WHALE or SHARK?
Was he munched up just like krill?"

"That simply isn't true," I say.
"And, hun, you need to chill."

"Did he go away on holiday?
To Barbados or Brazil?"

"No one has gone ANYWHERE . . .
And, hun, you need to chill."

"Is he at the zoo?

Is he at the fair?
Is he searching for a thrill?"

"Although we DO love the Ferris wheel . . .
Hun, you need to chill."

"But we're so confused!
And so concerned!
We cannot rest until . . .

We find out what has happened

to your older brother Bill!"

"Did he tumble down and hurt himself?
Have they given him a pill?

Is he in the pool or on the pitch,
Showing off his skill?

"There are NO hungry whales . . .

NO little green men . . .

Your hysteria is silly . . .

The truth is that my brother Bill . . .

Food

"Is now my sister Lily."

"It was maybe quite a shock, at first,
But she's really just the same.
She looks a little different
And she has a new first name."

"She's still clever and funny

and kind and cool.

She's really rather brill . . .

And if people have a problem we shout . . .

"HUN, YOU NEED

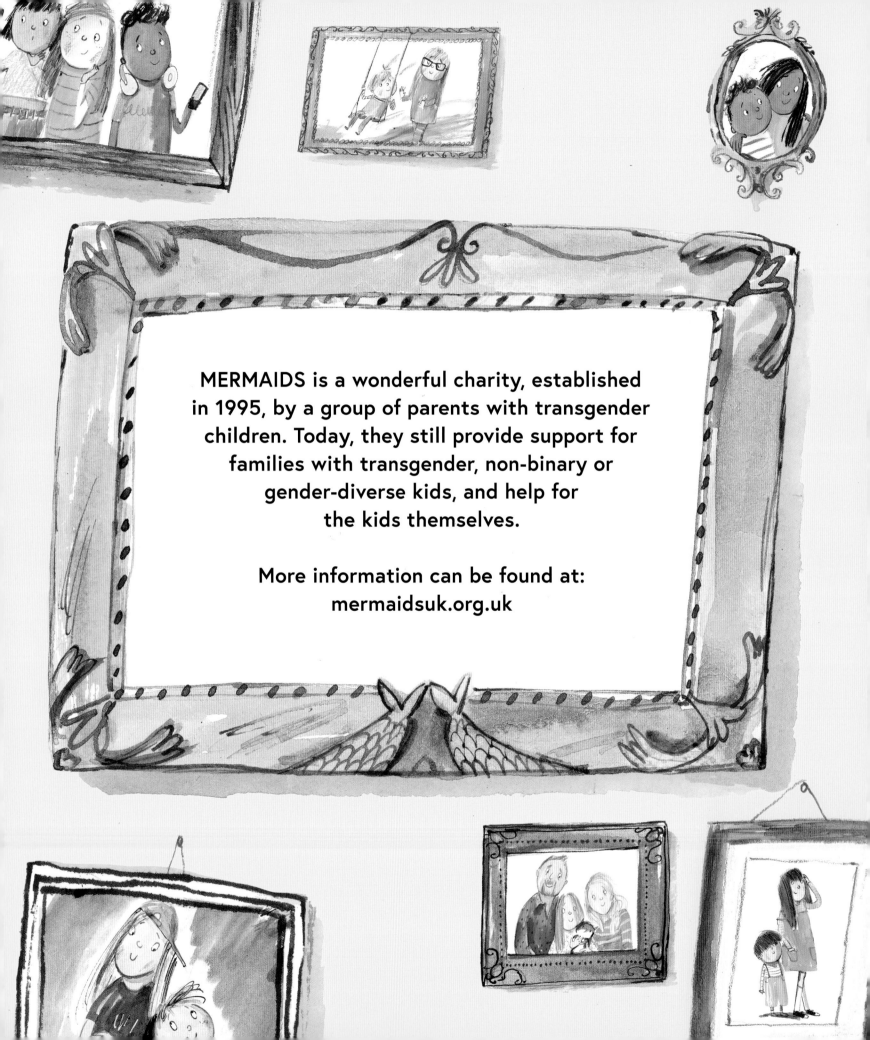

MERMAIDS is a wonderful charity, established in 1995, by a group of parents with transgender children. Today, they still provide support for families with transgender, non-binary or gender-diverse kids, and help for the kids themselves.

More information can be found at: mermaidsuk.org.uk